Dragged Up Through the Troubles

A Poetry Anthology

By

Liam Kelly

This collection is dedicated to:
Prison Arts Foundation

CONTENTS

FOREWORD

I've so many memories from childhood, growing up during the Troubles, and I feel relieved to put them somewhere. The number of lives I've seen destroyed because of bigotry, alcohol and gambling, everyone was looking for a way out. The pubs were never empty, the bookies were jammed packed, and everybody smoked. The catalyst was the Troubles, not only that, but we were kids fighting with bricks, broken bottles and petrol bombs. People didn't venture out of their own areas and survived in close-knit communities. People lived in each other's pockets, nobody had nothing but whatever they had, they shared.

Everyone was fighting for a cause, no matter what side of the divide you were on. What cause? We were just fighting because we were skint. My father would say 'we're collecting for the cause…it's *cause* we're skint.' Everyone laughed as if it wasn't real life. The characters back then were huge, larger than life personalities, charismatic. You almost felt invincible. But the reality was we woke each day to trauma, you opened your front door to riots. The constant, daily, thump, thump, thump of plastic bullets or crack, crack, crack of machine guns in the distance. You were striving each day to not end up as just another statistic on the 6 o'clock news.

I hope this sets a context for the poems.

Liam Kelly

80s Swingers Belfast by Patrick Devlin

KELLIO

I lived through the Troubles
In the shadow of death
Hell fires all around me here
Suckin' my breath
I look in my head and wadia' see
A sociopath, a psychopath and me makes three
We laugh in da moment
At dat moment in time
Cos rules doesn't matter here, livin' a crime
The hate for the Five O
The filth and the swine
Dopamaines, distortion of normalities fine
Am foamin' at the mouth like a rabid dog
A petrol bomb in one hand
Getting ready to lob
It soars into the sky and it's leaving a trail
A wave of destruction that's the final nail
Anger rage and suffering eating our lives
We grew up fast with nothin', sharpenin' knives
By the time that I was ten, I had a gun up to my head
Cursed to God almighty just to shoot me dead
This life is hell on earth, in a venomous scream
Can someone fuckin' wake me
From this post-traumatic dream.

MY HOMETOWN

Wee streets with cobbles
So dark and so grey
Streetlamps all busted
From riots an' affray—

Oul dolls with trolleys
Are rushed of their feet
Searching for bargains
To make tight ends meet—

A big pot of stew
On a wet winters night
Slopped into big bowls
For families just right—

The heel of a loaf
To soak up the juice
Pass me the hp
A dinner time truce—

Who's up for seconds?
My wee ma would shout
Get back in line son
And she'd give me a clout—

The olde days in Belfast
I remember so well
The riots and the Troubles
We were dragged up through hell—

We grew up with nothing
No materialistic things
But in Belfast in *them days*
We did live like kings.

PEACE WALLS

One thousand feet of barbwire fence
Surround our Belfast town
Fragmented minds, tormented souls
Supressed and pounded down

Corner boys, street to street
Long coats and tweed flat caps
The unemployed working class
Black smoking chimney stacks

Seven high-rise concrete blocks
Look out over jailed Belfast
Army checkpoints lookout posts
Peace Walls of hate, a mask

Memories soaked up into brick
And carved into their soul
For one square mile of murders
No counting what the toll.

Children's minds were bate and bashed
And stretched like rubber bands
Saw murders on these evil streets
Their minds like bare wastelands

Hemmed in like cattle, barbwire fence
In-between we tried
On lonely, bloodied Belfast streets
People lived and died.

2 Dozen by Patrick Devlin

ALL ALONG THE WATCHTOWERS

Barricades of razor wire
To rip you to a shred
No future for the Belfast boys
Was beat into yer head

Starved of air, toxic smoke
Fumes make lungs explode
Hands of time, a ticking bomb
Traditions to erode

Acid tongues incite and anger
To feed the hungry mob
Stamp fear on every cornerstone
Our lives to wreck and rob

Stop-n-search or snatch-n-grab
Stone blockades of six-foot square
For brutality and the torture
No human rights to spare

Our parent's fought tooth and nail
To ease their children's pain
To claim all Ireland's birth right
And smash the English Claim

The SS in their watchtowers
Encrusted in barb wire
Looked out over concrete jungle
Was poised to open fire.

THE WATER WORKS, NO RE-DO

How do people start again
When there's nothin' left to give
No love to show your childhood crush
From where you used to live

No squeezin' her soft hand so tight
While crossing busy road's
For every time she looked at you
Your heart and mind explode

We roll about the fresh cut grass
As sunlight blind's our eyes
Joking every chance we got
To deafening laughing cries'

We'd go and look for tadpoles
While wading through the streams
Push and shove and splash about
To shrieks aloud and screams

We'd dry off in the mid-day sun
Doing star fish on the grass
Slide down the hills of green so steep
Me and my merry lass

Head to toe in daisy-chains
With a flower in her hair
She'd never looked so beautiful
To know her was to care

I was ten, she was twelve
We'd close our eyes and pray
Our friendship was eternal
To forever and a day.

NO PEACE OF MIND

I can't escape that ticking sound
That beats inside my head
As self-destruction bomb goes off
That kill emotions dead

I've been near to death so many times
Too countless to recall
But something deep inside me died
For each and every fall

I hardened to the Troubles fast
By the brave old age of ten
As rubber bullets broke my bones
Eleven times back then

Bate with sticks with six-inch nails
The occasional wrought-iron bar
Was nearly kicked to death one time
My worst beating by a far

The daily suffering smothered me
For the childhood that I missed
Took cruel unusual punishment
Just trying to exist

Parents fought to feed their kids
As time's were hard all round
A massive bowl of buttery champ
Pork sausages stuck in mound

There was a girl just two streets up
I'd protect her to the end
My only saving grace back then
I married my best friend.

THE BUILD UP

Blackness suppressed so deep inside
Seeps out through tiny pores
Memories' ladened with pain and suffering
Silent screams, tormented roars

No one to hear our pleads for mercy
Cried God! Just ease our fears
No one came or saved or helped
As all fell on deaf ears

God? What God? What fucking God?
We scream inside our head
Do your worst as other did
Come strike us now down dead

Pain? More pain, more pain and suffering
Blanketed our wee lives'
As children of the so-called Troubles
Memories carved in brain by knives

We'd fall to knees with scream and cries
As battles were daily chore
Brutality dished out like bowls of stew
Starved kids can't eat much more

We're filled to brim with rage and anger
Burdened weight from memories' load
Brutally tortured and mentally scarred
Tiny childhood minds implode.

Back Up WHERE ARE YOU "Over" by Patrick Devlin

NO BELLS NOR WHISTLES

There are no bells nor whistles
No fancy motor cars
Streets so grey for us to play
Underneath the stars

Loads a bricked-up houses
The roofs have all caved in
Bricks and bottles and burnt-out cars
That streets were littered in

The laughs and cries of Belfast kids
Echoed through the night
Through alleyways and blood-soaked streets
brutality was so trite

We crept about and tippy toed
Like shadows in the night
We ran the streets and laughed and cried
'Til early morning light

We charged about our concrete lives
The violent lives we led
As Mas come out, to call us home
Only to get fed

Tears of joy and laughter's cry
Still flood our Belfast street
Just memories now that we relive
Now as adults when we meet.

There was no bells nor whistles
No fancy motor cars
Streets so grey for us to play
Underneath the stars.

WEE TOMMY TREACLE TRUNKS

Tension filled the hate filled street
Excitement gripped the air
Was gonna be the best riot yet
Our hearts and souls to bare

We gathered loads of ammo up
And planned this through the day
We shared a load a *Mars* bars out
To help work, rest and play

Now fully fuelled in starting blocks
'Get ready,' curly said
An ashtray hurled down from the flats
Smashed upon my head

My head exploded, pishin' blood
And I was knocked out cold
Woke up in hospital, two days past
Only to be told

'Ya missed a brilliant riot mate
We nailed em fucker's well
Twenty-five of us got shot
While giving fucking hell

We used up all our ammo
As we rioted thru the night
Wee Tommy tuck his nappy off
And tossed a massive shite'

'Tommy treacle trunks', I said
'Sure, he's barely to my knee'
'Well he shites just like a docker
Altho' he's just turned three'

'The soldier thought he got split
And rubbed it with his hand
He looked at it, had a sniff
He screamed and fucking ran.'

BLOODLUST

Blind fury anger bloodlust rage
Control our shattered lives'
Old scars reopened many times
Resealed by red hot knives

The sickness pulling at your heart
Mass electrodes light your brain
Watchin' loved one's dragged from bed
Adrenalin numbing pain

The stench of justice reeks of filth
And badness to the core
The corrupt and crooked powers to be
Seep puss from open sore

The dogmatic extremist partisan party
With supremacist bigoted views
The pack of fanatic zealots say
That liberal free thinkers loose

This catatonic state we're in
The foul stagnant air we breathe
Young half expanded burnt out lives
Where no one gets to leave.

Brown Sauce Sandwich by Patrick Devlin

WHO AM I AT 10?

Invisible enemies in my head
Shadows follow me everywhere
Disillusioned by normal life
Dark forces stalk and stare

A world of shattered sorrows
Is broke beyond belief
Death destruction at your door
The pain of anger and grief

Deep depression and despair
Everywhere I look
Decisions that were made for me
Bad choices that I took

My rage is uncontrollable
Silent assassins in my head
Can't take no more; on my knees
Come God and strike me dead

Heavy burdens pull me down
I can barely stand up straight
I'm really only ten years old
Feel death will seal my fate

No knight in shining armour
No Peace Corps to assist
Why is this a raging war
Can we not just co-exist

So, let us end our suffering
On both sides of divide
No bullets getting fired at us
And kids don't have to hide.

MA!

Horrific heinous homicides
Filed our heads with fright
Don't looked out the windows
Sirens wailed all through the night

Brothers and sisters huddled round
Warming by the fire
Ma *brung* in a loaf of toast
Our loving eyes admire her

Eight wee cups of steaming tea
All sweetened to our taste
Gone in 60 seconds flat
Even crusts don't go to waste

She'd sing to us her childhood songs
Doing actions and all that
Her madcap sense of humour
Had us laughing on our back

Our laughter drowned out sirens
Now fear can't grip and wreak
In our happy Belfast hovel
Our paradise so to speak

Treacherous murders lasted years
Our generation just flew by
I remember all the tears of joy
As I think of Ma and cry.

A BARREN PLACE

We dance between the buttercups
And fields of dandelions
Laughin' oh so very hard
We're very nearly cryin'

Tears of joy and rosy cheeks
We'd sit just holding hands
Blowin' kisses to each other
On these bloodied troubled lands

Darkened shadows everywhere
Fired shots all through the night
In treacherous murky Belfast streets
Kids white as sheets with fright

God just hear our prayers tonight
As we trembled to our knees
We beg God, to let us live
we'll be real good, so please!

Soldiers lined us 'gainst the walls
So everyone could see
And chained us up in leg-irons
At least our minds run free.

ARMOURED TANKS

Armoured tanks rolled down our street
And were poised to open fire
For interment had begun this day
Put men behind the wire

Their treatment was atrocious
No human rights in sight
Tortured, beaten to a pulp
As Union shows its might

The world looked on in horror
And were powerless to react
As English Nazi work camps
In H-Blocks, that's a fact

No rights or means to plead your case
You were stamped into the floor
No one to fight for justice
Excretion, our décor

Ten men had to starve to death
Before you all took heed
Screamed 'No' to prison uniforms
And definitely no force-feed

Your totalitarian grip on us
Your Marxist-Lenin state
As young people queued up to enlist
And history sealed your fate.

Half a Sixer by Patrick Devlin

CHILD VICTIMS

The psychodrama of old Belfast
Unfolds each night it seems
The reels replaying in my head
So vivid are my dreams

Another death in North Belfast
To screams that no one hears
Blood run outa children's wound
While holdin' back the tears

We fought to breathe and cried aloud
As kids protected streets
Left mental scars of all-sorts
mixed up like bags of sweets

Used, abused, left to right
Mood swings up and down
The victims of the so-called conflict
Not all beneath the ground

Untold damage overlooked
Kids pleads went unheard
We wanted to be children
Not frightened nor be scared

The story of a Belfast child
Has been told throughout the time
As terror ripped through Belfast's streets
Child victims was its crime.

CATA-PULT

Us *childer* hid in rubble
Our catapults in hand
Awaiting army foot patrols
Who walk on foreign land

We wait in deadly silence
Like a tiger stalking prey
To unleash a hail of ball-bearings
On this wet and windy day

Beads of sweat run down our back
Hearts pounding through our chest
Trembling, anticipation
Against our unwanted guest

We have them in our sights now
Our look out whistle sounds
They spot us in the rubble
They fire some baton rounds

While they were trying to reload up
Our ball-bearings hit the skies
Crash down with deadly impact
To feeble English cries

'What the fuck is going on?'
The English soldier screams
As foot patrols are shattered
Just like our childhood dreams.

HULA HOOPS

The children played on wastelands
Derelict houses all around
Broken glass and burnt-out tyres
Let strewn upon the ground

The girls had hula hoops
And bounced their rubber balls
Played skipping rope and tippey-tig
And chalked upon the walls

The boys had target practice
Played cribbie in the street
Had kick-the-can and rap-the-doors
Chelsea Whoppers for a treat

We had our no-go areas
The flash points so to speak
Where no one dared to go at night
Their future looked so bleak

Our encrusted barbwire playgrounds
Just like our dreams at night
Where innocent kids got laid to rest
A truly brutal awful sight

Shattered bits of boys and girls
Just lay amongst the rubble
If world can't see what's going on
By fuck, the youths in trouble

So give us back our childhoods
For us to have our dreams
So we can have a full night's sleep
Without those awful screams.

RAGE AND THE WAR MACHINE

Lives count for nothing here
A statistic on the news
As people they fall victim
To light another fuse

Rage now fuelled the war machine
And youth made us rebel
But nothing could prepare us for
The hate towards ourselves.

THE FEAR

Invisible armies in my head
Shadows follow everywhere
Disillusioned 'bout my life
Dark figures stalk and stare

A world of shattered sorrows
Lies broke beyond belief
Death, destruction at your door
The pain, the anger, the grief

Deepest darkest depression
It's everywhere I look
Decisions that I made for me
Bad choices that I took

Heavy burdens weighing me
Can barely stand up straight
I'm only fucking ten years old
Feel death will seal my fate

Crying out my deepest hurts
Can anybody hear?
So, we don't have to grow up fast
And kids don't live in fear.

STUCK IN THE MIDDLE

We were caught up in the grown-ups war
Where kids don't stand a chance
As tit-for-tat atrocities
Paramilitaries held their stance

This messed the mind up, of us kids
For we hadn't got a clue
Just had the willing to survive
But our hatred grew and grew

We rebelled against the world at large
For we had no other choice
As child soldiers of the Troubles
No one to hear our voice

This turned us into monsters
Barbaric and so cold
Sadistic savages of the war
The truth to now unfold

We charge in swinging hammers
To crush oppressors will
Threw bricks and bottles and petrol bombs
Our new adoptive skill

Risked life and limb most every day
'Twas normalised to us
As I look back at the Troubles now
For kids, was so unjust.

70s Street Corner by Patrick Devlin

A CRY TO GOD

Memories creep into my mind
While sleeping in my bed
Brutality shown from monsters
Filled us kids with dread

Not only Brits and Peelers
It was everywhere you looked
Stripped and whipped and beat about
The punishment you took

We learned so young to stand our ground
To look oppressors in the eye
And drive a spike into their ribs
Then watch the bastard's cry

We fought with chains and studded belts
Although we all looked frail
As bodies broke before their time
While parents rot in jail

Please God, please God just let me die
I can suffer no more pain
Just come and take me as I sleep
But leave my hate-filled brain

Then morning came you opened eyes
And breathed a happy sigh
If there was a God in heaven
He would have let me die.

STREET REARED

Street kids
Riotious mobs
Throwin' bricks
Lobbin' bombs

Dodgin' rounds
Fired from guns
Fuck we're flanked
Army comes

Dukin' Peelers
Turn da tide
Snatchies charge
Tryin' to hide

Tit for tat
How we roll
Vote for Sands
Flood the poll

History made
Thatcher's gaze
Sand's elected
From the maze

Mass hysteria
Across the land
Starves to death
By Thatcher's hand

Youth lined up
'gainst State law
Free the grip,
Of English law.

INNER PAINS

Voices trapped inside my head
Images haunt my dreams
My childhood mind imploding
To deafening silence screams

Chaos raining down on me
Dark shadows move around
Whisper wicked deeds to me
Bodies dragged along the ground

I see demons in the mirrors
Watching me watching you
And trying to control me
Don't know just what to do

Rage descends from heaven's high
The whole world is upside down
Psychosis seems to grip the horde
Pointed tails lash round and round

There is a devil growing inside of me
Horns cracking through my skull
This pain inside my fucking head
That never seems to dull.

BELFAST TOWN

This dirty old town of Belfast
What does she have to offer
No oil reserves or natural gas
To fill the English coffer

Wee parlour houses, tumbled down
To feed our kids we struggle
No kindred spirits here for you
Was she really worth the trouble

So what is it you really want
From our chimney stacks of peasants
There is nothing left but heart to give
To banish cruel suppressors.

Hail, hail the Brits are here by Patrick Devlin

NO ONE TO HEAR OUR CRIES

They break into our houses
Beat families to the floor
Off to rot in prisons
Can't take it anymore

Children watched in disbelief
Send shivers down our spine
Terrified we hide in corners
For our parents we did pine

Brutality was shown to us
As battered parents lay
Now we relive the trauma
The scars still deep today

Nightmares for us children
Keeps us up at night
For England's bloody war on us
A true horrendous plight

Dreams lay broke like most of us
As we cried ourselves to sleep
As we huddled in the corners
No-one to hear us weep.

THE BONE YARD

The bone yard is calling
She whispers your name
It's carried by winds
To extinguish a flame

Dark cumulous surround you
Build, encircle above
Now make way for buzzards
Picked bones here thereof

To gaze up to stars
A soft breeze on your face
To draw your last breath
Wait for death to embrace

No goodbyes to your loved ones
As you lie all alone
The hell hounds are snapping
At heels through to bone

A rough sawn wood box
No trim of white lace
Lies deep in the earth now
For trust you misplaced

In darkness you wallow
In a cold unmarked grave
As maggots start feeding
Your soul to enslave

The bone yard is calling
She whispers your name
It's carried by winds
To put out your flame.

TORMENTED MIND: MAN AND MONSTERS

Scratching days off a jailhouse calendar
Exhausted appeals make shackles heavier
The concrete pendulum of time drags me down slowly
A snail's pace, dark nights' nightmares
Stretching the strands of a lonely, tormented mind
Elastic grey matter, bouncing floor to ceiling
Wall to wall, a six-by-six closing in
A suffocating and smothered mumble of remorsefulness
A hill of jail beans drip fed for humane and moral fibre
Forced down your throat, rammed into your gut
And passed through a colon of low lives in denial
The putrid stench overwhelming
Blinding smells sickens me into a deep sleep
Hatred of fellow man and monsters
This dosshouse: Dung Beetle feeding on the depraved
A Volcano of vocabulary: vulgarness eats into my core
Of human decency and kindness
Scared to be scarred by the sickness that hangs heavy
I scrutinise, trying to see the deeds reflected in their eyes
Hoping and praying that when my time comes
To leave this God forsaken place; a hell on earth
I will see light shine on the face of goodness: humanity once
again.

LIBERTY FOR HENRY JOY

The society of United Irishmen
Led by Henry Joy
I'd spoke to him so many times
When I was just a boy

Wolfe Tone, Russell, Drennan
Done what no one dared
Converged with me while sniffing glue
In Clifton Street graveyard

LIBERTY EQUAL-LITY
We'd shout out from the crypt
Read Henry Joy's headstone out
As if it was a script

Hung for treason by the neck
In Cornmarket Square
In Belfast City centre now
Olde England deemed it fair

Henry called out for democracy
Which included all the classes
Of all religious parties
Presbyterian was the masses

The *Northern Star* paper said
Spread political manifesto
Formed secret armies in the North
No-one would have guessed tho'

I'd greet him with a handshake
Look him squarely in the eyes
Henry Joy it's been a pleasure
Here you and your sister lies.

TRAUMA

Guns n bombs and bombs n guns
Thunder 'cross the sky
As children look to heaven
It's not our turn to die.

INSECURITIES

We cry ourselves to sleep at nigh
While hiding under covers
No one to see our tears or pain
Not even our own mothers

Our nightmares lived in nightmares
That shuck us to the bone
While hiding under covers
And crying all alone

I still have vivid nightmares
Vivid pictures seem so clear
I'm just not under covers now
And trembling with fear.

THE HEARTBEAT OF A TICKING TIMEBOMB

Cockroach counting
Watching clock
Humdrum numbness
As I rock

To and fro
Upon my chair
Deafening silence
Every where

Heartbeat ticking
Pounding down
Struggling gasping
As I drown

Darkest down
Depth depraved
Soul destroyed
Can't be saved

Where darkness lives
And Demons thrive
In mass abundance
The Devil's hive

Entrails strewn
Guts and bone
Tortured mind
In jail alone

A single atom
In solitary cell
I wake on bunk
And still in hell

Same day everyday
Repetition
No name or number
No recognition

Thumb screws on
Of screw in gang
Pushed too hard
Now hear the bang.

DEEP DARK DEPRESSION DAMAGED GOODS

Depression bites savagely
Eating the last scrap of reason
In this fragile mind of mine
A heavy wet blanket suffocates
Suppressing me, drowning me
In self-worthlessness; heartbeat racing
Thumping through my chest cavity
Pulsating, deafening, bangs in my ears
Clawing, kicking and screaming I fight
For my own existence, apocalypse
In this sewer; of thrown away broken souls
Whose individual needs surpass
The needs of anyone else's bar none
Battle scarred and weary I carry on
Sick to the back teeth
Conformism, this humdrum life
My basic human instinct for survival races
To the surface, breaking from darkness
Through into darkness
There is no light ahead
And if by some great miracle
There is even one speck of normality left
By the end of my sentence
I will never be the same again—
I am damaged goods
My eyes blurred with sadness and pain.

COWBOYS AND INDIANS IN OLD BELFAST

Our wee town of Belfast
Blood soaked and rain
Wee small parlour houses
Whitewashed in pain—

Grannies in head scarfs
Wear shawls to keep warm
Natter on corners
Pass knowledge in swarm—

Bricked up *oul* houses
Half tumbled down
Makeshift toy forts
Kids roll on the ground

Laughter and tears
For this cold lonely place
Burning busses for roadblocks
Separate interface—

Cars burnt out, abandoned
Still smouldering on fire
'Cos this was our playground
Stench of rubber from tyre—

We played Cowboys and Indians
Fierce Apache we'd choose
Just like the underdog
You don't want them to loose—

We danced round our campfire
Used our fingers for guns
Shot each other and fell
Complete madness for fun—

A few minutes later
We were back on our feet
Cowboys and Indians
Wild West was our street.

SUICIDE IN JAILS

My heart beats
To a distant drum
Far off lands
As I succumb—

Dark fear in dreams
Of tortured souls
Walk these jails
In shackles roam—

Dark spirits trapped
Half-way Hell
Corpses dragged
From their cell

Rigor sets
Cold as ice
Against the system
Self-sacrifice—

Duplicate forms
Complain to screw
Doing your wack
No judicial review—

Heartless; cruel jails
Men in their prime
Slice open veins
One last time.

80s Street Corner by Patrick Devlin

I AM AN OLDE RED BELFAST BRICK

I am a brick
An olde red Belfast brick
I cast no aspersions
Nor tell no lies
I do not judge
For I am impartial to all
Like the rains that quenched this once green fertile land
I have laid witness to countless murders
Torture and inhumane atrocities
By evil and brain washing regimes in its concrete jungles
Both sides of the divide attack
Turn on each other hatred inbred
I have been used in street-to-street battle
Saw streets run red with innocent blood
AND I WEEP
I weep for the poor souls who lost their lives
And cry empathy out for their love torn families
Father against Father
Son against Son
Saw devastation and destruction far beyond recompense
Burnt out cars
Bricked up derelict houses
Used as children's playgrounds
Fear and worry lay heavy on furrowed brow
While tears flood family homes
And as I fade through time
Like distant memories of the past
I see the poor tortured and diminished soul
of Belfast drain

For I am as old and as wise as old Belfast itself
I have shed many tears
My head hangs low in shame.

THE ABYSS

The abyss stares back into the void of emptiness
To a dried and withered husk of a shell
The dream of dreams, relived over and over again
Plucking at my heart strings
A blinding shining light engulfs me
And wraps me in the wings of a celestial being
Heavenly euphoria ignites every brain cell
Sending a tidal wave of heartfelt emotional tears
Drowning me in love that once was
My eyes open and I scream
I scream why, why, why, dear God
Just let me sleep
I lie here a heaving wreck of a person
Incapacitated and lifeless
Please God just let me sleep
The hip-hip-hip-hip-notic rhythm beating in my head
Her laugh ever so sweetly calls and beckons me
Like a moth to the flame, I follow
Lulling me into absolute peacefulness
And tranquillity numbing all the pain
My heart pulls me closer
She urges me closer still
There's is no way back for me
My jail bunk is my oasis now
And my 6 by 6 cell is my castle
Danger to all ye who enter here
Beware! Wild dog at large!

GHOSTS OF THE INNOCENTS

The rough and murky waters
Surround this green grass isle
As death squads bloody head count
Leave bodies in a pile

Some couldn't have an open coffin
Coroners went by dental charts
Mothers' hearts get ripped from chest
As they buried body parts

My son, my daughter, my beautiful child
How could they do this onto you
Hacked and chopped or blew apart
Innocent victims you were too

Ghosts of innocent victims
Roam Belfast streets at night
Reliving their last moments
Never out of families' sight.

MIRRORRORRIM

I stare at myself
Scrutinize line and wrinkle
Eyes fixed on eyes
I search my soul
For the sick and depraved deeds
Forgiveness is futile
Skeletons in my closet scream—

I try to quash my mind, torn battlefield
Decayed and maggot ridden corpses'
Torment and browbeat
My soul, these ghostly figures
Squeal and taunt
Inciting fear and dread, subliminal—

Can anyone see these atrocities of mine?
As I wait for the fire and brimstone
A wrath of fury raining down
In biblical proportions—

I've waited a lifetime for redemption
It's buried so deep for fear of reprisal
For who else can see into the window of my soul?

I've asked many times, for torture
These are my crimes
I'm cursed to damnation
Until my last breath
The heartbroken families—poor souls bereft.

If it Bleeds by Patrick Devlin

FIRST CHRISTMAS CEASEFIRE 1974

Curly and the gang and I
Could not believe our ears
The RA had called a ceasefire
Reducing us to tears

Us kids can have our Christmas
For the first time in our life
British troops withdraw their might
Easing all the strife

We still sat round our campfires
Telling jokes to fill the cracks
That the paras had beat into us
And Loyalist attacks

Us kids were truly kids this time
No pressures bearing down
No Army firing point blank range
No weight of English crown

We showed the world what we could do
Though loyalists had their guises
By adding more atrocities
Incendiaries and devises

No tit-for-tat that Christmas
No rioting on the streets
Our Christmas stockings ripped apart
And filled with Christmas treats

Tears of joy and laugher
Fill my Belfast home
Let us enjoy our childhood
And leave us kids alone.

SHANGRI-LA

I stare out of the prison cell window: the bars, the brick walls encrusted in razor wire…they dissolve away like two fizzing Cocodamol, to reveal a tropical paradise. My eyes almost exploded as they fill to the brim. Shangri-La unfolds before me, lust crisp green grass so tender underfoot, in the soothing pool dew trapped between my toes. A beautiful marble fountain trimmed in gold. I bathe in it's cool, youth rejuvenating waters. Palm trees intermingling with fluorescent flowers which I'd never seen before. My lungs are filled to capacity with all the wondrous aromas. Endorphins rage through my brain like an out-of-control forest fire. I bask in true freedom: no borders, no boundaries or probation.

BANG! The cell door slams shut, my heart nearly explodes, palpitations race through me as the screw shouts, 'LOCK UP.' I was furious and I could feel the anger and resentment building against the system and the regime. When the dust finally settled, I drift off, calming myself.

I am a wild animal locked in a cage. You may incarcerate me and throw away the key, but my mind is an entity onto itself and runs free like the might Amazon River. It is more powerful than a tornedo gathering momentum. It is unstoppable, as the mightiest tsunami. The electrode encephalogram can only be measured on the Richter Scale.

My mind roams the universe: a ghost, a free spirit and can never be broken.

ABOUT THE AUTHOR

Liam Kelly was born in Belfast in 1965 and grew up on the New Lodge Road, North Belfast. Liam was knocked down accidentally in 1973 and has no early childhood memories. He woke up after a three-month coma in 1974 and the only person he recognised was his granny. When he got out of hospital, he stayed with his aunt in Glengormley for ten months. On returning home, he experienced a baptism of fire when he walked out his parents' front door and into the middle of a full-scale riot on the streets of Belfast. At 9 years old Liam was convinced he was a giant, due to having to return to primary one at school in order to learn to read and write again.

The Troubles profoundly impacted on Liam's early childhood and the levels of rage seemed all encompassing. Liam joined the Merchant Navy in 1980, and this was another major turning point in his young life. Liam married his childhood sweetheart, Denise, and they had two children, Lia-Marie and Chei. Liam credits Denise as his saving grace, she saw something inside him that nobody else could see. Denise brought these qualities to the forefront and turned him into a loving husband and father. Sadly, Denise died in 2017 from cancer and her loss profoundly affected Liam's mental health.

In July 2018 Liam was arrested and spent 20 months in custody where he began writing poetry and stories. He credits Prison Arts Foundation with guiding him on this path as a writer and jokes about never having read a book until he went to prison. Liam is an award-winning writer and poet, receiving Koestler Arts awards for his writing as well as prizes at the prestigious Listowel Writers Week. His writings have been published in *Time In* magazine.

Printed in Great Britain
by Amazon

26269729R00040